To our dearest
June and River
and all kids
who love hugs.
XO

Published and distributed in the United States by: Hay House. Inc.: www.hayhouse
.com® • *Published and distributed in Australia by:* Hay House Australia Pty. Ltd.:
www.hayhouse.com.au • *Published and distributed in the United Kingdom by:* Hay
House UK. Ltd.: www.hayhouse.co.uk • *Published and distributed in the Republic
of South Africa by:* Hay House SA (Pty). Ltd.: www.hayhouse.co.za • *Distributed in
Canada by:* Raincoast Books: www.raincoast.com • *Published in India by:* Hay House
Publishers India: www.hayhouse.co.in

Illustrations and Book Design by: Michelle Polizzi — designbylovelyday.com

Hardcover ISBN: 978-1-4019-5172-6

10 9 8 7 6 5 4 3 2 1
1st edition. January 2016

Printed in the United States of America

WORDS BY
NY TIMES BEST-SELLING AUTHOR
NICK ORTNER
AND **ALISON TAYLOR**

The Big Book of HUGS

A Barkley the Bear Story

PICTURES BY
MICHELLE POLIZZI

A short, short time ago in a forest really, really
close to home, Barkley the Bear awoke with a startle.
He heard Mama and Papa Bear in the family room.

"BARKLEY!"

his dad called.

Barkley pounced into the family room.
"Happy birthday, Barkley!

TODAY IS THE DAY,"

Papa Bear said with a grin. "You are now old enough to join
the family business of giving hugs and spreading love."
Finally! Barkley had been waiting for this day since he was a little cub.

As they set off, Barkley started to feel a little nervous. "Papa, wait . . . What if I'm not good at this? What if I can't help everyone?"

Papa Bear smiled at Barkley. "Son, I worry about that every day. To get ready to give others the love they need, I start with the first hug of the day. Hugging yourself gives you the confidence to share the love you have!"

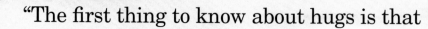

"The first thing to know about hugs is that

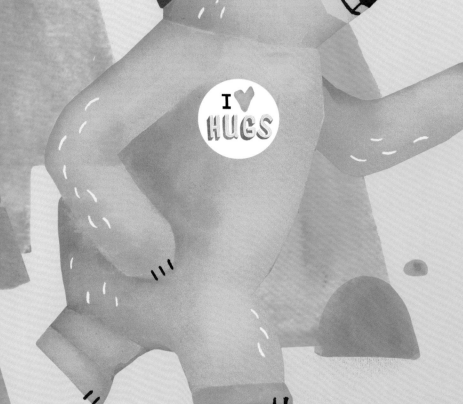

HUGS A

and can be given at any time.

When you give a hug, you are wrapping your arms around the heart. The hug you give depends on what that friend needs, and it's up to you to figure that out!"

I ♥ HUGS

Papa Bear added, "The second thing to know about hugs is that . . .

"...HUGS ARE EASY TO GIVE

when words are hard to say. Now and then, people have a hard time coming up with their words, like *'I'm sorry'* or *'I'm upset,'* so we use a hug instead!

Let's find out what kinds of hugs we can give . . ."

I ♥ HUGS

Papa Bear whispered, "If you see a close friend before they see you, it's fun to give a surprise hug."

RY the rabbit CHUCKLED in surprise!

Papa Bear continued. "If you haven't seen a friend in a long time, you can give a long hug. Or if you are saying good-bye to someone you may not see for a while, it's the perfect time for an *extra, extra, extra* long hug."

longer . . .

longer . . .

longer . . .

"Sometimes friends give a hug with a

KISS ON THE CHEEK!

That is their way of saying hello or good-bye.
This happens more if you travel outside this forest."

"Oui! Oui!"
announced Oscar the
french bulldog.

"If two friends need a hug at the same time, you can hug both together! We call this the pickle-in-the-middle hug. It's fun to be the pickle!" Barkley giggled as he watched.

"I want to be the pickle," mentioned Mabel the moose.

"I love trees!" beamed Barkley.

Papa Bear moved closer to a tree as he said,
"Humans help take care of the forest and keep it safe.
They cherish this place so much, we call them tree huggers!"

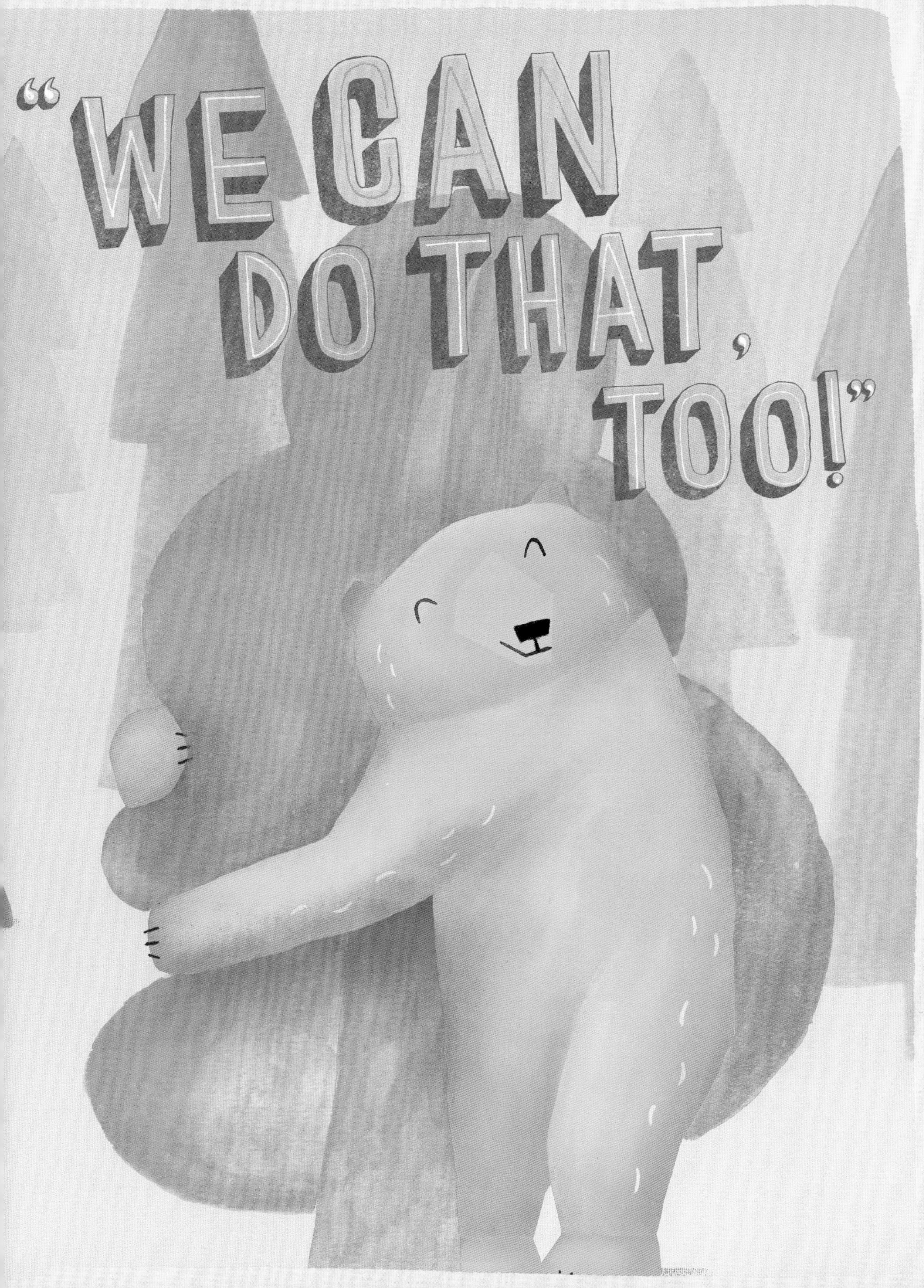
"WE CAN DO THAT, TOO!"

"Little friends like the tornado hug because it's fun. Pick them up while you hug and twirl around! Be careful when you put them back down, just in case they're

DIZZY!"

Barkley practiced his twirl to look just like his dad's.

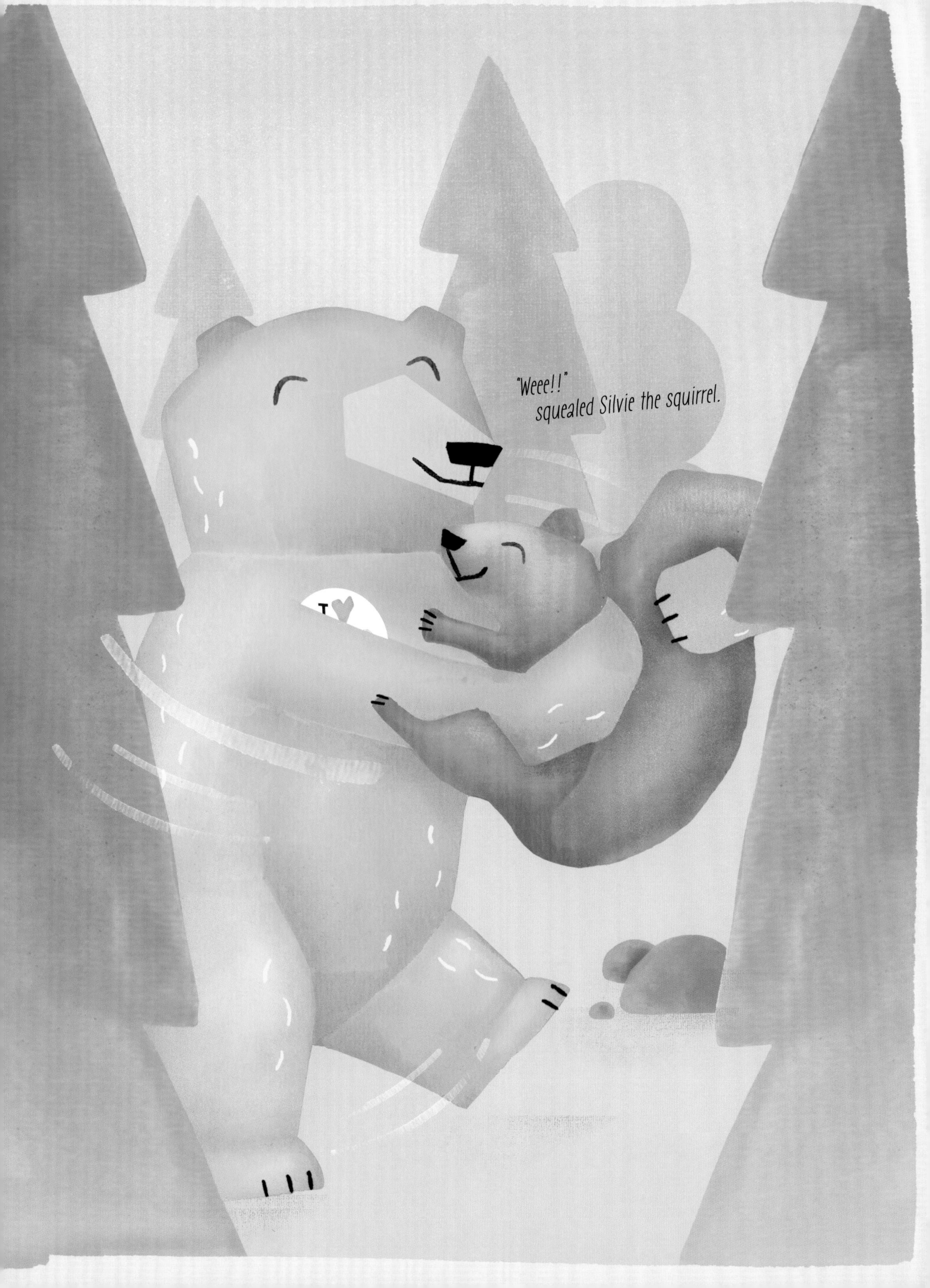

"Weee!!"
squealed Silvie the squirrel.

"Sometimes I'll do the pick-me-up hug when I'm excited to see someone. It's like the tornado hug without the twirling. Make sure to get those toes

OFF THE GROUND!"

"Papa," said Barkley quietly. "What about that friend?"
He pointed toward a big tree.

"Yes, you might come across someone who doesn't
look like they want a hug. Asking if it is okay to give
a hug is a good idea. They may say 'yes,' but there
are times that they would rather just be alone."

"I feel the love . . ."
said Pete the
porcupine.

Papa Bear put his hand on Barkley's shoulder and said,
"They know how much you care, but they may not want a
hug right then. That's okay. You can think about them and
give them a hug in your mind. That means just as much!"

Papa Bear and Barkley continued through the woods, paying attention to the friends around them. "If you have a lot of friends you want to hug at once, it is a good idea to do the group hug!" Papa Bear told Barkley.

"As sweet as honey!" buzzed the bees.

"There are times when you give a hug that you don't want to let go, and you squeeze harder and harder. That's called the squeezer. Make sure you don't squeeze too hard!"

"Keep squeezing!" suggested Olivia the very wise owl.

"Hey, guys!" Papa Bear called out to some other papa bears who were helping to build a fence.

Papa Bear turned back to Barkley. "Boys have special hugs they like to do. We call them the pat hugs. We shake hands first, hug, and pat our friend on the back."

"Buds for life!"
bragged the papa bears.

As nighttime approached, Barkley looked around and saw all the
happy animals in the forest. He turned to his papa and said,
"Even though hugs don't cost anything . . . you still get a lot in return!"
Barkley thought for a moment. "How do you know when the job is done?"

Papa Bear answered, "The job will never be done because friends need hugs whether they are sad, mad, or happy. No matter what someone is feeling, everyone needs a hug . . . But look around, and you'll see that we're done for the day."

"WAIT! *We're not done yet!*" Barkley exclaimed. "Papa, I can't
believe you forgot the most important hug of all! Our specialty hug . . .
The one where you have SO much love to give that you wrap
your arms around someone you love and squeeze tight . . . tight . . . tight.

THE GOODNIGHT BEAR HUG!"

Papa Bear smiled proudly at Barkley. *"I love you, Barkley."*

"I love you, Papa."

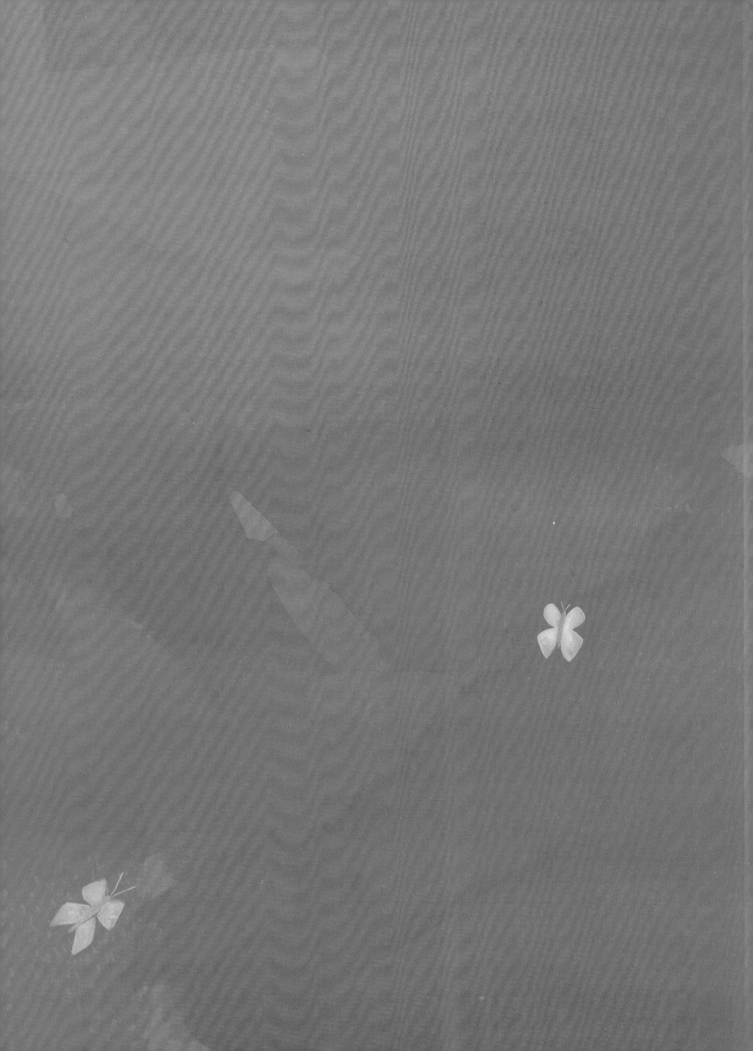